This is a work of fiction. There are some references to historical places and characters to make the story more compelling.

ONCE AGAIN

First edition. July 1, 2020.

Copyright © 2020 Theresa Vernon.

To my family who always inspires me to create new projects

Chapter 1

After the disastrous Kent marriage proposal, Elizabeth was furious. Still, she didn't understand why she also felt an emptiness in her whole being. Her headache got so intense it was impossible to conceal sleep. The thoughts of what just happened and how she was so wrong about the notion Mr Darcy had of her kept her awake almost until dawn, when she finally succumbed to slumber.

After leaving the Parsonage, Mr Darcy was unable to face any of his relatives at Rosings Park. He decided to go directly to the stable to organise his thoughts and calm his anguish. He couldn't understand what went wrong. Any lady would welcome his address and would feel flattered by his proposal. Surely it was an honour for any gentlewoman from his station. So even more for someone as beneath him as Elizabeth. Anger was soon replaced by uncertainty and pain. Darcy, being a man of action, immediately started to think about how to solve this problem. He concluded that Elizabeth was never going to accept him. She detested him in such a violent way that it would be impossible to change her mind. Although he was hopeless, he didn't want her to remain with the mistaken opinion of what happened with Bingley and Wickham. At least, he needed justice.

He rode back to Rosings since it was getting dark, and it would be difficult to explain to his demanding Aunt, why he was riding at such a strange hour. He went directly to his chamber and started to write a letter to her. After several hours of writing different versions, he came to the best possible explanation of his "crimes".

The next morning he was able to find Elizabeth walking through the park, and when she was behind a grove, he reached her. His pain was even more significant when he saw the sad expression of her beautiful eyes. *Was she also affected? Of course*, he thought, *she is a generous person*, not that she cared for him, but surely she felt some "charity" or "pity" towards him. He didn't want her pity; he only wanted her love. After some minutes of hesitating, he was able to place in her hand the long letter and immediately left. Elizabeth stood frozen, unable to react about what happened, and saw him go, thinking they would never meet again.

Chapter 2

With summer, also came some happiness for Elizabeth. Her favourite Aunt and Uncle, the sensible Gardiners, invited her for a tour in the North. They were going to visit the Lake District and some northern counties. They were leaving in a fortnight, and she was keen to start the journey. Her spirits were not completely lifted, but she was usually a lively young lady, so she was excited about the change of scenery and the excellent company.

The journey started, and her Uncle, Mr Edward Gardiner, gave her disappointing news. Due to the arrival from a vital shipment, they would have to shorten their trip to three weeks instead of six weeks, and they could not go as far as the Lakes. Nevertheless, they would visit many fantastic places, especially in Derbyshire. Elizabeth went pale with the sole mention of the name, which didn't go unnoticed by her intelligent Aunt.

After visiting Nottingham, they started the journey to Lambton. Once the subject was on the table, her Aunt

Madeleine mentioned that Lambton was only five miles away from Pemberley.

"Lizzy, I remember you mentioned last autumn you had the fortune to meet Mr Darcy of Pemberley," said her Aunt.

"Yes, I don't know if fortune is the right word, Aunt," replied Elizabeth.

Her Aunt, sensing that there was more to the story than Elizabeth wanted to divulge, subtly continued to press the subject. "I would say with certainty, fortune. I remember his parents quite well. They were honourable people, the best masters, and very generous with their tenants. I even remember Mr Darcy as a boy. He was charming, although shy, and so handsome."

Elizabeth couldn't believe this torture. Of course, he was handsome, honourable, and now she understood; he was also timid. But it was too late for her. After reading his letter, she realised how she missed the best possible opportunity in her life. To find a man who would care for her would not be easy. Besides, she would never find someone who admired her and loved her so much as he did. Elizabeth was convinced she lost this chance forever.

Her Aunt didn't miss the changing expressions on Elizabeth's face, but being as prudent as she was, didn't mention a single word about it.

It was late afternoon when they were close to Lambton. It was sunny but very humid. They couldn't know how the unpredictable weather in Derbyshire was dramatically changing into an intense summer storm. They were on the main road, closer to Pemberley than Lambton, when the thunderstorm started. Suddenly, a bolt of lightning scared the horses, and the coachman lost control of the reins. The carriage drove out off the road, down a hill, and overturned. With the force of the crash, Elizabeth flew out of the carriage. Afterwards, all was darkness.

Her Aunt and Uncle were hurt and couldn't get out of the carriage. Mr Gardiner was unconscious, and Mrs Gardiner had a broken leg. The coachman was lifeless on the ground. The rain started to pour, and almost half an hour passed until a tenant boy found one of the wheels close to his farm. He was curious and began to walk up the hill when he saw the broken carriage.

He first found Elizabeth. She was soaking and almost unconscious. He immediately put his small jacket to cover her wet chest, and she gave her a meaningful look and a sweet smile. Paul was immediately enchanted with her since, even though she was so wounded and in pain, she was so thankful to him. She could barely talk and asked him about her Aunt and Uncle inside the carriage. He went to check on them and then back to Elizabeth. Paul told her they were not seriously wounded and avoided any mention of the coachman. He promised her he would return with some help. Paul, the tenant boy, decided that he needed help from several strong men and a doctor. It was wiser—although a little farther—to run to Pemberley than to return to his farm.

Once Paul arrived at Pemberley, he was attended by Mrs Reynolds and narrated that an elegant family had an accident and needed the Doctor. Mr Darcy, who was residing at Pemberley, heard some commotion coming from the door and went to see what the matter was. He congratulated Paul on his efficiency to seek expert help and asked him to accompany the rescue team. Mr Darcy, feeling, as usual, responsible for what happened in his premises, or close to them, also decided to be part of the rescue team. But before leaving, he asked Mrs Reynolds to have Paul change his extremely wet clothes.

In a matter of fifteen minutes, the group departed and arrived at the place of the accident. First, they found the Gardiners, who were trying to maintain as warm as possible. Mr Gardiner had already regained consciousness but was unable to get out of the carriage to help his niece. Some of the men started to help them out of the carriage. In the meantime, Paul asked to go with the Doctor to where the gravely wounded beautiful lady laid. Darcy, Dr Scott, and Paul went further, hill down and saw the wet figure lying on the ground. They were silent, the scene was shocking, and all feared the worst. They got closer, and then Darcy could not believe his eyes. He startled the moment he recognised her, and called her, "Elizabeth!" His mind and heart betrayed him. He couldn't call her differently. For him, she was just Elizabeth. She barely opened her eyes; she didn't know whether it was a dream. She was in acute pain, freezing, and almost unconscious. The Doctor quickly examined her to determine the best way to carry her. Once he determined that her spine was unhurt, he said she could be brought to the carriage but very carefully because she seemed to have some broken ribs. Darcy did not hesitate a single moment and carefully took her in his arms. Dr Scott, who knew Darcy since he was just a boy, immediately understood this was "the woman" Fitzwilliam Darcy loved. He was pleased to see that finally, the taciturn and aloof Darcy was in love but was extremely concerned that this young lady would not survive. That would be one more tragedy in Fitzwilliam's life, who suffered so much after his mother, and then his father passed away.

Once inside his carriage, Darcy placed her on the couch and gently started to take off her pelisse. He dried her face with his handkerchief, took off her gloves, and put her cold hands in his to give her some warmth. The Doctor and Paul also rode with them in complete silence. They witnessed the depth of admiration Mr Darcy had for the beautiful lady.

The rain was still heavy when they arrived at Pemberley. Darcy entered his ancestral house with her in his arms and, with his commanding voice, immediately indicated Mrs Reynolds to place Miss Elizabeth and his relatives in the family wing. A quizzical look between Mrs Reynolds and Dr Scott went unnoticed by Darcy. Mrs Reynolds followed behind and could see his Master's desperate look, so she was limited to obey. There would be time afterwards to ask some questions and understand the whole situation better. Still, she started to suspect that this lady had something to do with the sadness her Master faced in the recent months since his arrival from Kent.

***

Once in her guest room, he laid her on the bed and reluctantly left, so Dr Scott, with the help of Mrs Reynolds, could examine her. He went to check on her family and on Paul, who was having some supper in the kitchen. Once again, Darcy thanked Paul for his smart choice of coming to Pemberley directly instead of going to his farm. Although closer, the capacity to attend wounded persons would be limited. Paul was proud of himself, and mentioned that he hoped the lady would recover. He said that she was like a forest fairy, with her beautiful hair and eyes. Darcy, feeling the stress of the past hours, couldn't contain some tears. He genuinely feared that once again, he could lose Elizabeth. Not that he had some hopes before, but now he realised that she may not survive the accident, and he felt that all his assets, his position, his wealth, and his name were worthless. The boy sensing his inner turmoil hugged him. He told him what, in his childhood naiveté, he said to Elizabeth, "Forest fairy, please don't close your beautiful eyes. You brighten the forest with them. Promise me, you will not close your eyes, and she promised. Even though she was lying under the rain for so much time and injured, she kept the promise, and she still had her eyes open when we rescued her." Darcy didn't know why, but the boy's words gave him some hope that all was not lost yet.

After the touching conversation with Paul, Darcy returned to the family wing to see the Doctor's hypothesis. He knew she was grave, to say the least, but could only hope that her love of life would help her recover. He approached her room and waited outside until Dr Scott finally came out. "Miss Elizabeth was severely injured, but there is hope." He continued describing her injuries. She had a dislocated shoulder, which should be attended immediately with some extra help. Her right leg had several scratches, which had already been cleaned, she also had a small contusion near one of her temples, and she had three broken ribs. He was still waiting to ascertain any possible damage to her right lung. That would be the most severe risk for her health, plus the fact that her body temperature was low. He feared some possible pneumonia could develop in the coming days. Darcy didn't hesitate a moment and immediately came to the room. When he entered the chamber, he was shocked to see her fragile body in the beautiful bed. He imagined Elizabeth in Pemberley for many months already, but never in his thoughts would he have known that she would be there like this.

He came closer to her and dared to touch her hand, which was still cold. He took it in both his hands and remained in quiet communion for a while. Dr Scott and Mrs Reynolds watched the scene in front of them with sorrow and prayed for his Master and his lady.

Dr Scott interrupted him after a while since it was of the utmost importance to have her shoulder rearranged. He required the help of three men to hold her. The process would be excruciating for her, not only because the procedure was painful but also because of the broken ribs. Mr Darcy, of course, was to be one of the assistants. He would hold her other arm and hand, while two of the most loyal footmen were holding her feet.

"Miss Elizabeth, please stay still; it will be less painful," the Doctor said.

"Mr Darcy?" she was looking in disbelief at the scene in front of her.

"Shh, all will be fine, you are in the best hands, and we will take care of you, please do as the Doctor says."

Then, Mr Darcy and Elizabeth's eyes met for a moment, and he could see some tenderness in her look and a small smile that brightened her face. "I trust you," was all she said.

At that moment, Dr Scott proceeded to correct the shoulder. The pain was severe, but Elizabeth was a strong lady and didn't scream. She squeezed Mr Darcy's hand with unbelievable force and then lost consciousness. He held her hand for a while and then wiped her sweating forehead with a cloth and left the room.

After he left, he went to the chamber where Mr and Mrs Gardiner were being tended to and greeted them. He was positively impressed with their manners and was happy to see that they were going to recover soon. They asked about Elizabeth and mentioned that as soon as they were able to be with her, they will help in her recovery. That would have to last a few days since Mrs Gardiner was already showing signs of a cold. With the fear of pneumonia, Dr Scott didn't permit her to visit Elizabeth in her chambers.

***

Mr Darcy didn't want to sleep in his chamber; he absolutely didn't want to sleep. He would sit down in an armchair beside her bed, but that would be improper. "Propriety be hanged." He went from his room to Elizabeth's. She was being accompanied by Mrs Reynolds and Sarah, Georgiana's maid. He was pleased to see that Mrs Reynolds was personally involved in her care. He considered her more than a loyal servant; for him, she was like a mother. He entered the room and sat beside Mrs Reynolds, who was sitting next to the bed. They did not speak, but words were not necessary. He communicated his feelings, and she understood him.

After a while, Mrs Reynolds said, "I see you will not be able to sleep and would rather supervise our patient directly. Sarah will remain here for proprietary reasons. But you will also have to rest at some point in time. It will make no good to her if you also fall ill."

"Dr Scott also said that due to the broken ribs, we should apply ice packs for the first two days, and she also needs to be moved every three hours to prevent lung infection. If she is awake, she should do some gentle coughing exercises. We both determined that you will be required to perform these tasks since you are strong but gentle," she said this with a knowing look on her face.

"Of course, I would not have it any other way, you know." That is all he replied. He took Mrs Reynolds place, to be closer to her. Once again, he took her hand and prayed. After a while, all the tension of the day washed over him, and he also fell asleep. When the time came to change Elizabeth's position, Dr Scott entered the chamber and woke Mr Darcy up. He explained how he should place himself behind her and gently lift her and change her position. He did as instructed, and she remained asleep. In her sleep, she could feel strong and caring arms, but she didn't open her eyes.

Mr Darcy stayed all night with her, changing her position every three hours, as Dr Scott instructed. The next morning he was tired but happy to be able to help the most important person in his life besides his sister Georgiana. Darcy did it without expecting anything from her; it would be too much to ask. Nevertheless, he couldn't forget her words to him, "I trust you." That simple sentence nourished him and kept his spirits up for the new day.

Mr Darcy couldn't neglect his other duties. After taking a bath and breaking his fast, he went directly to his study to manage his estate affairs. He also sent for Paul. Darcy wanted to have him visit Elizabeth and see how she was much better than before. Mr Darcy kept visiting Elizabeth that day every three hours. She was still sleeping, but the Doctor was optimistic about her progress.

After two days, Elizabeth regained consciousness, and Mrs Reynolds was ecstatic. She was dreading the worst and was suffering for his Master. Elizabeth was perplexed about her whereabouts. Mrs Reynolds explained about the carriage accident and Paul coming for help. Elizabeth asked for him since she was sure she owed him her life. If he hadn't found her, she would have died that day. Mrs Reynolds asked Sarah to fetch Mr Darcy, Dr Scott, and then Paul.

Once Mr Darcy heard that Elizabeth was conscious again, he stood from his desk and went with long strides to her chamber. His heart was pounding, and he thanked God for the miracle of having her back. Darcy hesitated to enter the room, not knowing her reaction to him. She was kind to him, while she was almost unconscious, but he didn't know if it would still be the case, once Elizabeth realised where she was. When he entered, Dr Scott was smiling at her, and they were in deep conversation. *"Oh, how I love her,"* Mr Darcy thought. Before she saw him, she felt him and turned to face him. His eyes met hers, and he was rewarded with one of her friendly smiles. Before, he never saw her smiling at him like that. He was bewitched, once again.

Mr Darcy approached them and greeted her. She immediately started to thank him for all the hospitality and dedication of the staff, she was honestly grateful. Dr Scott continued his conversation explaining Elizabeth her wounds. The Doctor said she would have to stay in bed for at least a week since her broken ribs were an issue that needed to be handled with care. "Speaking of care, you will still be helped to change your position in bed every three hours, like we have done so far, with the help of our best nurse in the house."

"And who is this nurse? I cannot remember who has helped me so far."

Dr Scott couldn't help but chuckle, and Mr Darcy pointedly looked at him. "Mr Darcy, of course, he would not allow anyone to touch you for fear of having you hurt." Elizabeth and Darcy awkwardly looked at each other.

"Miss Elizabeth, as you can see, Dr Scott is more impertinent than a young lady of Hertfordshire, we both know. You must understand him, no?" She started to laugh, but her painful broken ribs didn't allow her to continue. "Please, take care, I am sorry, I caused some pain," he abruptly said.

She placed her hand over his to comfort him and said, "Do not fret Mr Darcy, I am stronger than I appear."

"Of that, I am a witness!! And speaking of witness, I asked Paul, the boy who saved you, to come and say hello. He was enchanted by you and has been asking every day about you."

"He is the sweetest boy I have ever seen. He came to help and even gave me his jacket to protect me from the weather. I will not forget him, how could I?"

Mr Darcy left to fetch Paul. They both came to her, and she felt some tears coming without control. She couldn't believe that such a small, simple farm boy could be cute, smart, and generous. Paul was reluctant to enter the chamber, and Mr Darcy took his hand and helped him come in. Once inside the room, he said, looking directly at Mr Darcy, "Master, I knew the forest fairy would recover."

"Paul, it is so nice to meet you again. You saved my life, you are an angel, I will never forget."

"No, Miss, you are the angel and the Master has been very kind to me, it was nothing." After giving him her thanks and having some small chat, she was exhausted, and Darcy noticed it, so he decided to leave her. Paul and Darcy left the room, so she could sleep again.

***

Late that afternoon, Elizabeth was restless. She wanted to get out of bed; she felt a strange boost of energy. She was at that moment alone with Sarah and asked her to help her. Sarah didn't know what to do. She knew the Master would not like it since the Doctor gave clear instructions that she would stay in bed at least one week, but on the other hand, she couldn't disobey the young lady, who was Mr Darcy's friend. Reluctantly Sarah helped her get out of bed. Elizabeth went to the window; she needed to see the outdoors. Being indoors was oppressive for her.

Elizabeth was watching the beautiful view from the window when a gentle knock was heard. Sarah fret. As she predicted, Mr Darcy was standing on the doorway. His look of surprise caused Sarah to gasp. Elizabeth turned around and greeted him. "Elizabeth, you cannot be out of bed, it is not ..." His voice sounded commanding. Elizabeth was angry with his high-handedness.

"Proper?" she finished for him. "Well, it wouldn't matter since I am just tolerable, not handsome enough to tempt you, no? I could also be improper . . ." She was feeling hot and dizzy and couldn't understand her harshness.

Mr Darcy was barely able to reply, "You are more than tempting, you already know that. I was going to say it was the Doctor's instructions for your recovery." At that moment, Elizabeth started swooning, and he ran to her and took her in his arms. He carried her to the bed, and his anger was immediately replaced by concern when he noticed how warm she was. "Fetch Dr Scott, Sarah, immediately." Sarah left the room at once, and in some minutes, the Doctor, Sarah, and Mrs Reynolds entered the room. Darcy was kneeling beside the bed and touching her forehead. The Doctor froze with such a scene, fearing the diagnosis. He approached the bed and asked Darcy to leave the room.

Mr Darcy knew what was coming. The Gardiners suffered from a severe cold, even though they remained the whole time after the accident inside the carriage. Elizabeth was exposed to the cold and wet weather for far too long. Once again, his spirits sank, and he went to his study to think. Think about what could have been, about his parents, about life and death. He remained there, standing and staring from the window for a long time. He didn't realise how much time passed and didn't notice the arrival of Dr Scott. When the Doctor called him, he turned and didn't like what he saw. It was evident that the diagnosis was not optimistic. "I thought that she would recover from her wounds, and we would be so lucky to avoid pneumonia. Her fever is very high, and she is still weak. She needs to be supervised twenty-four hours, as we have been doing, but there is no guarantee of the outcome. We must keep her hydrated and be careful about her temperature. I will start with some medicine to help her, but her state is delicate. You know I will tell you to rest, and I also know you will stay with her regardless, so go to her." Darcy didn't reply and silently left his study with a heavy heart.

"*How could this have happened?*" He was confident that she was already in the path of recovery. She was young and healthy; her passion for life captivated him from their early acquaintance. He prayed that those aspects of her personality were enough for her to recover. He felt helpless but could not leave her. Not now, not ever. He would be with her for as long as God let him. He thought that he could give her part of his strength and feel she had a purpose. She couldn't leave so soon, not like this. Not before they could talk again, and he could see her beautiful eyes and warm smile.

Mrs Reynolds and Sarah were nursing Elizabeth, who started to regain consciousness. She was restless and began to whisper to Mrs Reynolds. "I need to talk to him; I need to apologise."

"Please rest, Miss Elizabeth, you need all your strength to recover, you need to calm."

"No, please, I can only rest after I apologise to Mr Darcy."

After her insistency, Mrs Reynolds left the room. She went for Mr Darcy, who was already on his way to see Elizabeth. He entered the room with some trepidation. He sat near her bed, and she looked at him. It was painful to see her feverish eyes, but he would be strong for her. Her voice was weak but firm. "I am so sorry. I was again rude to you. You have been so kind, and I have been so ungrateful. I am so sorry I treated you in such an unladylike manner. Please forgive me, so I can rest in peace."

Those last words were too painful to hear, he could bear it no longer. He couldn't stay on the chair; he needed to be closer to her. He sat on the bed and took her hand in his. He looked at her with all the love his lonely heart had and then placed a kiss on her palm. "There is nothing to forgive, dearest Elizabeth. You taught me a tough lesson about humility and humanity. I deserved your words, and I hope we will have plenty of time together. I am glad you can rest now, but I will be waiting for you to recover. I need you, and I love you more than life itself. Please don't leave me." She closed her eyes, and he could see a lonely tear running on her face. With his other hand, he wiped it, and she opened her eyes and smiled at him. His heart skipped a beat, and deep inside, he prayed all would be fine.

***

He remained with her during the night. He tended her with the help of Sarah. At this point, he didn't care about propriety at all. She had nightmares throughout the night. She barely talked, but he could understand some of her anguished words during those feverish nightmares. "It is so dark and cold, I have fear." He tried to calm her by holding her, telling her that she was safe, that she would be fine. His words soothed her, but sometimes he didn't know if she knew he was there, but he talked to her in such tenderness, that Sarah was hardly controlling a sob. His dutiful and honourable Master deserved to be happy. She was very close to Georgiana and knew that both siblings needed a lot of love. Although she hadn't had the chance to speak that much with Elizabeth, she immediately recognised a generous personality. So different from the young ladies of the "ton" that usually went after poor Mr Darcy in such a blatant manner. She was already charmed by Elizabeth and recognised the true love Mr Darcy had for her. She decided to help him as much as possible so that Elizabeth would recover.

They frequently placed a cold cloth on her forehead, he gently brushed some curls from her face and temple, and Sarah often went to change the water, so it remained always chill. During the second dreadful night, when they were moving her, Elizabeth whispered, "Don't leave me . . ."

"Never my love," said Darcy. She hung close to his chest, and he didn't dare to move for a while. Only when he felt her steady breathing, he gently placed her on her pillows.

When morning came, Mr Darcy and Sarah were confident that the fever would subside. Nevertheless, it took two more days for Elizabeth to recover from the fever, and to the Doctor to finally report that she was out of danger. Mrs Gardiner was almost recovered from her cold, and her leg was improving. She was desperate to see Elizabeth and was finally able to accompany her during some time that day. Elizabeth was immensely glad to see her Aunt. Her Uncle was also improving but still had a severe cold so she couldn't see him for a couple of days. Elizabeth's path to recovery was excellent, and Mr Darcy was feeling a relief like never before. He wasn't sure whether once Elizabeth would be healthy again, she would react differently to him. But Mr Darcy was a very persistent and obstinate man. He had already decided he would do everything to convince her to become his wife. It was impossible to imagine life without her, not anymore. And after having Elizabeth already in Pemberley, he wasn't willing to let her go. At least, not until he heard directly from her what her wishes were.

Chapter 3

One lovely afternoon, Mr Darcy and Mr Edward Gardiner were sharing a glass of brandy in Darcy's study. In the last days, they have become quite close. Mr Darcy admired Mr Gardiner's intelligence and excellent company immensely. He was surprised how before Kent, he had such prejudice for Mrs Bennet's family. Not that he could understand how this real "gentleman" was that lady's brother. "I need to return to London in a couple of days. You have been extremely generous, but we need to return home. I also have important business to attend, so I need to plan this with you." Mr Darcy didn't want them to leave.

"Dr Scott has the last word on this, but Mrs Gardiner will still have an uncomfortable carriage trip to London. It is a long journey. There is no rush, you are more than welcome to stay here as long as you wish."

"Mr Darcy, Madeleine, is a strong lady. But you are right; we will follow the Doctor's orders for her and Elizabeth."

"Considering that Miss Elizabeth's condition has been more delicate, Sir, you should allow her to stay longer to recover."

"Mr Darcy, I understand your concern," he said this with an arched eyebrow, knowing already Darcy's feelings for his niece. "But we cannot abuse your hospitality, and it will also be improper to have her as a guest at a bachelor's house."

To avoid a moot discussion, Mr Darcy suggested they have a conversation with the Doctor to understand the best course of action. In the meantime, Darcy received a couple of letters. One from his cousin, Colonel Richard Fitzwilliam, who was really like a brother to him. The other was from his sister Georgiana, telling him that she would be arriving soon at Pemberley for the summertime. Having Georgiana together with her widowed companion could be an option for keeping Elizabeth at Pemberley. It wouldn't be improper.

On the other hand, having Richard teasing him about how deep in love he was could be a burden. He laughed to himself about how foolish he was. If Elizabeth could stay, he could tolerate anything, even his "annoying" cousin.

Before dinner, Dr Scott joined Mr Darcy and Mr Gardiner, and they discussed the condition of his patients. The Doctor expressed that it would be ideal to have Mrs Gardiner at least for a week and Elizabeth for four more weeks. Her broken ribs would limit her capacity to have a carriage ride for at least that time. Mr Darcy was relieved! Mr Gardiner was concerned but understood. Mr Darcy suggested that Mr Gardiner could ride to London first and that Mrs Gardiner could remain with Elizabeth until they would be ready to make the journey. He also offered that he accompany them back to London since he would soon have some business in town. That solution suited them all, and it was settled then.

***

The next morning Elizabeth woke up better than before and was happy to see that she could get out of bed without help. She was proud of her progress and wanted to show it to Mr Darcy. During those feverish nights, Elizabeth knew and felt the love Mr Darcy had for her. Even when she seemed to be unconscious, she knew it was him who cared for her. It was overwhelming to still be loved by such an honourable man. She wanted to show him the effort she placed into her recovery. She was doing it for his sake as well as for her. She asked Sarah to help her find out where Mr Darcy was. She returned to the room in a couple of minutes, telling her that he was working in his study. Sarah helped her with her hair and with a simple morning dress. She started to walk, it was still painful for her, but she managed with Sarah's help. They gently knocked on his door. "Enter." Sarah opened the door for her, and she stepped in. He looked up and couldn't believe Elizabeth was standing there.

Darcy almost ran to her and took her hand and placed it on his arm.

"Is this a good idea?" he said.

Elizabeth started to laugh, "I think this is the best idea I have had in years. I wanted to thank you and show you how much my health is improving. And what better way than walking even if it is indoors." He gave her one of his charming smiles. She could only stare at him and his lovely dimples. "Mr Darcy, I have it in good authority that you look great when you smile. My goal from now on is that you will be smiling more." He could not contain his laughter. Sarah was astounded to see how Miss Elizabeth was able to make the Master laugh. She had never seen it before in her years of service at Pemberley. What an incredible lady!

That afternoon, Elizabeth felt much better after being able to walk and talk in such a friendly manner with Mr Darcy. She decided it was time to inform her best friend about the events of the past weeks. She dreaded Charlotte's response, but she needed to confide in her as well.

Dear Charlotte,

I am not even sure how to start this letter. Many things have happened in recent months that I fear I will not be able to organise my ideas and feelings.

Well, I will start with my last days in Kent. I will also confess that I feel distressed because I have to accept that you were right from the very beginning. You have always been so smart, but I was blind and prejudiced, so I could not recognise what I know now for a fact. Mr Darcy was in love with me almost since our acquaintance in Hertfordshire last autumn. He didn't stare at me to find fault, as I was quite convinced. He was attracted to me. Oh, Charlotte! And he proposed to me that evening at the Parsonage when I did not attend Lady Catherine's invitation. Yes, you will also be quite angry with me. I refused him, Charlotte. His proposal was a complete disaster. He made it in such insulting terms for my family and my station in life, it was humiliating, and I lost my temper.

I didn't reason at the time, and I behaved terribly. I insulted Mr Darcy in such an awful way that I feel ashamed of myself. But that is not the worst of it, Charlotte, the hurt in his eyes was shocking. That look haunted me for months. But that is not all. The day after our terrible fight, Mr Darcy apologised and gave me a letter. I know I shouldn't have received it, but it was so quick, I didn't have the time to react when I had already the letter in my hand, and Mr Darcy was already gone.

Charlotte, once again, I completely misjudged him. He explained a lot of things about some unjust accusations I made. I should tell you in person since one of them is of a delicate nature, but suffice to say that your sense was above reproach. Mr Wickham told many lies to the people in Meryton. After reading his letter, I was able to understand the greatest mistake of my life.

For several months I thought I would never see Mr Darcy again. But after a horrible carriage accident in Derbyshire with my Aunt and Uncle, we were rescued by Mr Darcy himself. Fate has a strange way of placing people together. Charlotte, I have already been two weeks in Pemberley. I have also seen the constancy of Mr Darcy's admiration for me. Even though I was cruel to him in Kent, he has been so generous, and he has expressed he never stopped loving me, and will never end loving me. I cannot believe it myself.

I wanted to share the happy news, I know he is patient with me, but I hope to confirm soon that I am being courted by the only man I can love.

*Your friend
EB*

Chapter 4

Unfortunately for Elizabeth, all the correspondence Charlotte received was intercepted and read by her husband, Mr Collins. As a clergyman, Mr Collins was devoted to God, but even before God was his patroness, Lady Catherine de Bourgh.

He was shocked and resentful by hearing his cousin Elizabeth would aspire so high above her station. Mr Darcy was not only the nephew of Lady Catherine, but Mr Collins had always heard from the formidable lady that Mr Darcy was engaged already since being an infant to his cousin, Ms Anne de Bourgh. So, the first thing he did after reading that letter was to head directly to Rosings Park to show the offensive missive to his patroness.

Miss Georgiana Darcy arrived one day before Mr Gardiner's departure. In the beginning, she was a little nervous about the encounter with these visitors. Georgiana heard from her brother back in autumn about a Miss Elizabeth Bennet. She was sure she was the first lady in which his brother showed some interest. She hoped the lady would be someone special, she feared his brother would either choose a fine lady from the "ton" or succumb to Lady Catherine's wishes.

The moment Georgiana was greeted by his brother, she was stunned. She never remembered seeing his face so relaxed. He looked different in a positive way. "Georgie, how good to have you back home," he said. "I am so happy to have you here with me. And that you will finally meet Miss Elizabeth and some of her family." They went to the morning sitting room, where Elizabeth and her family were reading. Elizabeth's health was improving, but it still had a long way to go; she couldn't stand up quickly from the settee but greeted Miss Darcy with a warm smile. Georgiana was delighted to see this lady's gentle and kind manners and felt a great relief to confirm that his brother had chosen so well.

***

As the days went by, the friendship between Georgiana and Elizabeth grew stronger. Georgiana was happy to share her music knowledge with Elizabeth and even started teaching Elizabeth how to improve her drawing skills. The highlight of this period of bliss was the arrival of Colonel Richard Fitzwilliam, the favourite cousin of both Mr Darcy and Georgiana and also one of the guardians of the latter.

Richard was more than a cousin to Darcy, he was his closest friend, and they were actually like brothers. He was so happy to see his taciturn cousin, who had so many responsibilities in life, to have found such a lively partner. The Colonel would promote the match with his father, Earl of Matlock, and sister of Lady Catherine. Richard knew his father would not readily accept someone with the lack of connections Elizabeth had, or even worse, with links to trade. Still, he also knew his father and mother placed more importance on the fact that Darcy needed someone special. His cousin needed a kind and intelligent woman. Therefore, Richard decided he would start his "campaign". He felt confident about being a good strategist.

Unfortunately, some good things in life don't last long. One beautiful July morning, Elizabeth was reading on the terrace when an express came from Longbourn. At that moment, she was alone since her Aunt and Georgiana went to Lambton to buy some art supplies. Elizabeth read the note in complete disbelief. She would never have thought that her sister Lydia and Mr Wickham could be fond of each other.

Dear Lizzy,

I am sorry to send you such terrible news while you are recovering from your accident. Still, the most distressing situation happened while Lydia was in Brighton with the Fosters. Last evening the Colonel came to visit us to inform Papa that they have eloped.

Can you imagine! Mama is now in bed, Papa has already contacted our Uncle Gardiner to help him find them. It seems that Mr Wickham had some significant debts and needed to flee, and he found in Lydia some excuse. We don't think Mr Wickham loves Lydia, even worse, it seems that Mr Wickham is not the gentleman we once thought he was.

I pray you could come back to Longbourn as soon as the Doctor allows you to travel. In the meantime, please pray for us.

Your loving sister,
Jane

To say that Elizabeth was in shock is an understatement. As soon as she read the letter, she was shivering terribly. She felt her hopes crashing. How would Mr Darcy accept such a family? He was right from the very beginning about the unsuitability of the Bennet family. At that moment, Mr Darcy came to accompany Elizabeth for a while. In the last weeks, she spent a lot of time with Georgiana, which gave him pleasure, but he was always looking forward to some private moments with her.

He knew every expression of her. He had studied all her mannerisms for a long time and was immediately aware that something terrible happened. He rushed to her and embraced her with such tenderness that Elizabeth could not tell him the awful news. They stayed like that for some time, and then she handed him the letter. The shock in his eyes was evident, and Elizabeth's spirits were crushed even more. She understood the helplessness of it all.

But Mr Darcy was a man of action, used to handle complicated situations, and had already faced something similar. His mind started working immediately towards the steps to be taken. He gave her assurances that he would be able to find Wickham. He even confessed he felt partially guilty for not warning the good people of Meryton, including Elizabeth's father, about who the real Mr Wickham was. She gave him comfort, assuming a part of the guilt and reassuring him that she understood the need to protect Georgiana's reputation. Nevertheless, Darcy was not feeling blameless at all.

He left her to find Richard reading in his study. It was good to have him there. He related the situation to Richard, who became furious with Darcy for not finding a way to protect Meryton's people from the scoundrel, who he hated more than Bonaparte himself! "Darcy, how could you have done nothing at all! This is not acceptable, you should have warned Colonel Foster in a discreet way and the poor merchants of that town. You should have told me Wickham was in the militia, and I could have helped somehow. This is a disaster." Darcy couldn't agree more and looked so hopeless that Richard also felt pity for him. Things were going finally in the right direction for Darcy. This stupid action of the reckless sister would put a massive obstacle for his future with Elizabeth. Richard slapped him on the back and assured him, "We will rescue this girl, make Wickham pay for all his past sins, and you will marry Miss Elizabeth. I promise." Darcy just gave him a sad smile.

After an hour, Richard and Darcy left Pemberley to help Mr Bennet and Mr Gardiner with the search. Darcy left a note to Georgiana explaining briefly that he and Richard had urgent business and asked her to keep taking care of Elizabeth.

In the meantime, the news of Lydia's behaviour could not be contained in Meryton's small town, thanks to Mrs Bennet's nerves. Mr Bennet had insisted his wife remain quiet of the whole affair to protect Lydia and the girls. Unfortunately, Mrs Bennet needed to talk to Mrs Lucas, the mother of Charlotte Collins, and one of her closest friends.

That is how the news also travelled to Kent and Lady Catherine. Unbeknownst to Charlotte, her letters continued to be intercepted by her husband. Charlotte was in shock after hearing the news from her mother about the elopement and the consequences for Elizabeth's future with Mr Darcy. That would change things dramatically.

Chapter 5

While Darcy and Richard went to London in search of Wickham and Lydia, the most unpleasant visitor arrived at Pemberley. Lady Catherine arrived at the manor on a sunny morning. Mrs Reynolds knew that Mr Darcy was a very private man. He would not have told his Aunt about Elizabeth and the current predicament, which Mrs Reynolds somehow intuited.

Upon her arrival, Lady Catherine started giving orders to the staff, Mrs Reynolds included. She demanded to see Elizabeth. "Where is that insolent girl? I will be very displeased if she doesn't come at once." After a couple of minutes, a nervous Elizabeth arrived in the parlour, where Lady Catherine sat like a queen. But Elizabeth being Elizabeth, did not feel intimidated at all. At least not at the beginning of the conversation.

Unfortunately for Elizabeth, Lady Catherine was also an intelligent woman, who already knew Elizabeth's personality and came with another strategy to convince the upstart of leaving Pemberley. "Miss Bennet, how fortunate you could be taken care of here, after your accident. I wouldn't expect less from my nephew, but it is a relief to see you so well recovered." Elizabeth did not trust these "friendly" words and decided to remain quiet. Seeing that she had an audience, Lady Catherine continued, "You will be at no loss about why I am here. We both know that my nephew is a noble gentleman. Of course, he also has noble blood, but his essence is what makes him superior and noble. I assume he has already proposed. And now that you have seen him at his best, here at Pemberley, I can imagine you will be glad to be his wife." Elizabeth replied that she was thankful for his generosity and all the help provided for her recovery. Still, she wouldn't presume about her nephew's future plans. At this, Lady Catherine replied, "My dear Miss Bennet, we are both intelligent women. I have seen my nephew with you when you visited Kent and also have knowledge about his care for your welfare, so let's be honest with each other. He plans to offer for you if he hasn't already done so, but it is a blessing you were able to see the circle in which he moves. You have seen the great responsibility he has as a Master of this grand estate and the importance of continuing the legacy of many generations. You also know that your family, your connections to trade, and lack of fortune will have a very negative effect in his life. And this will be a burden for his future children, and even Georgiana." Elizabeth was silent and remembered the bitter words Darcy himself said to her at Hunsford Parsonage back in April.

It was overwhelming to hear them from someone else, and the worst is that deep inside, she felt Lady Catherine was right. To be the "right Mrs Darcy", there were several requirements Elizabeth lacked. She was aware of the sharp difference in their stations, although she also was from the gentry. Lady Catherine, astute as she was, continued with her line of arguments. "Besides, you can imagine that in the beginning things will look bright and rosy, but you know these differences instead of decreasing tend to be more noticeable over time. But the worst obstacle is that Mr Wickham will be your brother-in-law." That was the final stroke, and Elizabeth was speechless. Seeing the effect she had in Elizabeth, Lady Catherine decided that the deed was done and invited her to have some tea.

After a quiet half an hour, Elizabeth asked for permission to return to her room, claiming she was still having some headaches. Lady Catherine happily obliged. Once in her room, she ran to the bed and cried until she fell asleep. Later that afternoon, Georgiana and Mrs Gardiner returned from their visits at Lambton to find a satisfied Lady Catherine reading in the library and Elizabeth nowhere around.

When Mrs Gardiner entered Elizabeth's chamber, she saw the sadness in her countenance. Elizabeth woke up and narrated her conversation with Lady Catherine and her fears about the unequal marriage she would have. Mrs Gardiner insisted that having known Mr Darcy for a while, she thought they had an excellent chance to live a happy life. Still, Elizabeth was stubborn and asked her Aunt to return to Longbourn to help her family, especially Jane.

The following morning, Elizabeth and Mrs Gardiner started their journey south. Lady Catherine was quite satisfied, and Georgiana was very sad but understood Elizabeth's desire to be with her mother and sisters during this time. She didn't know that Elizabeth had decided never to return and was moved by the sad farewell she gave her, Mrs Reynolds and Dr Scott. Elizabeth asked

Georgie to deliver her letter to Mr Darcy and a note to Paul. She didn't think this was unusual since she had felt that his brother and Elizabeth already had an understanding. It was a hard letter for Elizabeth to write, and she departed Pemberley with a broken heart.

***

In the meantime, Darcy and Richard were able to locate Wickham after a couple of days. He was living at Mrs Younge's boarding house with Lydia. Once they were sure of their location, they informed Mr Bennet and Mr Gardiner about it and decided the best course of action. Mr Bennet was too distraught with the situation, so Mr Gardiner, Richard, and Darcy went to intercept the couple, accompanied by two of Richard's most trusted aides. It was an unpleasant scene to see the lack of decorum and selfishness of both of them.

Mr Gardiner couldn't believe that one of his nieces would go that far but was also aware of how spoiled Lydia was. He tried to reason with her without any success because she was convinced of Wickham's love. Richard insisted that Wickham was only trying to escape from his debtors and that she was easy prey. "Miss Lydia, as soon as he finds a way out, he will leave you without any remorse, don't you see? There is only suffering if you stay with him. Darcy has a beautiful state in Scotland, and you can stay there until this scandal disappears." Lydia couldn't be convinced and turned to Wickham for reassurance. She was shocked when she heard him say, "I will be happy to leave her for another, I am growing tired of this child, and would be glad to do so, for ten thousand pounds."

In that instant, Lydia's world seemed to come to an end. Mr Gardiner reacted furiously towards Wickham and punched him in the face. Thanks to his military experience, Richard was able to control the situation. He was enjoying seeing Wickham's pretty face swollen and his nose broken. But that was not the time to lose control. Lydia cried, and Mr Darcy, with his usual self-control, tried to calm her. Richard was thinking about how to get rid of Wickham and find a suitable solution for this predicament. Tying Miss Lydia to this scoundrel would be a terrible solution. However, it would be a divine punishment for Wickham and the traditional way to handle this matter.

That instant, Richard remembered one of his fellow young officers from a respectable family. He also required funds and could also be strict enough to tame the wild child. "Wickham, we will review this option you desire. In the meantime, Miss Lydia will go to Mr Gardiner's house, while Darcy, you and I make some arrangements," Richard said.

Darcy eyed him quizzically but knew that showing doubts in front of Wickham wouldn't be a good strategy. So he let Richard lead the conversation. "This is the plan, Wickham. You stay here under the supervision of my aides. At the same time, I go and have some discussions with a potential suitor for Miss Lydia. I am not sure if he accepts, but if that is the case, we could give you two thousand pounds and a position in the Navy with one of my friends, Admiral Livingstone. That is all we will give you, plus your promise never to put your unpleasant presence in England again." Then he indicated to Darcy that they could leave.

After they left the boarding house, Darcy dared to start talking, "Richard, if Miss Lydia does not marry. The family will be ruined, and Elizabeth will not be willing to marry me. How could you open that door to him? I am surprised by your generosity with *my* money."

Richard broke back in, "Calm down cousin, I am trying to find the way for you to marry Miss Elizabeth. Don't you see it? If Miss Lydia marries Wickham, Elizabeth will not accept the sacrifice you and Georgiana will have to make if he becomes a member of the Bennet family? We need to find a better way to get her out of this situation. Miss Lydia will be your sister, how can we have her marry such a monster?"

Darcy had to concede that he was not thinking clearly. It was so good to have Richard with him. He was desperate to solve the matter, but desperation usually leads to wrong decisions.

Richard told Darcy he already had someone in mind. The fourth son of a tradesman, Lieutenant Graham, was an intelligent, hard-working officer. Richard valued him and thought that if he married a gentlewoman, it could be an improvement in society for him. There was great potential for him to ascend in the military. On the other hand, Graham was kind but quite strict, exactly what Lydia needed. During the carriage ride to Darcy House, Richard told Darcy more about Walter Graham and was agreeable with the plan. Even though the Lieutenant came from trade, this was much better than having the steward's son and rake as his brother-in-law. The part of the idea that didn't convince either of them was to have Wickham start a career in the Navy and risk . . . future problems. He could come back after a few years and wreak havoc again. Also, Wickham was a deserter, and Richard had to report him to his commanding officer. That was the only possible solution with Wickham.

Richard left Darcy at his house and proceeded to the barracks to find Lieutenant Walter Graham. He presented the idea to him. At first, Graham was reluctant to tie his life to a girl who most probably has lost her virtue, but more concerning to him was her personality. He agreed to meet her first. Based on how this meeting went, the Lieutenant would make the final decision. He was not afraid of naughty little girls. Having three younger sisters, he knew how to treat them. But other things were necessary to find in her future wife. It was a good offer in terms of money, which could be very helpful for his large family. Most importantly, he trusted the Colonel and was loyal to him.

So, the day after that, Richard, Darcy, and Lieutenant Graham arrived at the Gardiners House. Mr Bennet's first impression of the officer was positive. He hoped this could be feasible since marrying her daughter to a wicked man was not an option he was willing to accept. Miss Lydia arrived at the sitting room dressed in a beautiful age morning dress. She was a beautiful girl, and after hearing the cruel words from Wickham, she was also somewhat subdued.

Nevertheless, if she didn't find anything attractive in the officer, things would be more complicated. Lieutenant Graham was not as dashing as her George, but he did have an imposing countenance. He was taller than Wickham, had a grave voice, and exuded authority and virility. He was definitely attractive and handsome enough to tempt her.

The Lieutenant was happy to see that she had a sensible Uncle and intelligent father. Still, he was also impressed with her beauty. All the Bennet girls were beautiful. Jane was a classical beauty. Lydia was very similar to Jane but with darker hair and a livelier countenance, which would make her the "beauty of the family" if she improved in her manners.

They had an awkward conversation at the beginning. Miss Lydia, weighing the limited options she had, started to be more her usual self, extrovert, and full of zest for life. That was something the Lieutenant wished in life, a little carefree spirit and more liveliness. So it was set that they would wed in five days once the special licence was procured. It would be a quiet affair. The couple would have to depart immediately to Newcastle, which would also help to patch up the scandal.

With this arrangement in place, Richard and Darcy departed to the unpleasant dealing with Wickham. At the boarding house, he was as nonchalant as usual. Wickham thought to have the upper hand. Little did he know that since Richard had to report him to his commanding officer, there was already an arrest order for Wickham as a deserter. So, even if Darcy was willing to offer him some funds to leave England for good, it wouldn't be possible now, and in the end, it was the only way to act. In their consciences, they could not offer freedom to a deserter of the country. They were witnesses of Wickham's arrest, who couldn't believe until the last minute how his plan went so wrong.

***

An exhausted Darcy left the boarding house. It was sad to see that someone with the opportunity to improve his station in life was so consumed by envy. George Wickham was his childhood friend, and this closure was hurtful, no matter how much damage he had done to him and the people he loved the most. Richard accompanied the recluse to be sure he was adequately imprisoned. Darcy still had one unpleasant errand to perform before leaving for Pemberley. He was desperate to see Elizabeth again and tell her the positive outcome. Darcy didn't want to write about it, it was better to tell her everything in person and propose. They had lost so much valuable time; he wanted her in his life soon.

He owed Bingley an explanation of his meddling back in November and decided to go directly and visit him. Bingley was pleased to see him again and immediately noticed the severe demeanour of his older friend. It was a blessing that Bingley was alone at home. His annoying sister Caroline was visiting some friends in Sussex, so Darcy could speak freely. They went to Bingley's study, where Darcy happily accepted a brandy. "Bingley, I have been postponing this meeting, but now it is inevitable." Bingley raised an eyebrow but kept quiet. "I might have been wrong about Miss Jane Bennet. I have it in good authority that she is shy and doesn't express her emotions openly. She was glad to receive your attentions and had feelings for you. I misjudged you and her, and I am sorry for any suffering I caused you both."

Bingley shifted in his seat and replied to this confession with something unexpected, "Darcy, since when you know this, why are you telling me now?"

Well, it was time to confess everything. "I know since April, and I am telling you now because I was a coward and left Kent since I could not bear the refusal of the woman I love." Now Bingley was curious! "I proposed to Miss Elizabeth in Kent." It was hard for his pride to tell his friend this part of the story. "She rejected me. During her refusal, we talked about her sister and my meddling in your relationship. She was quite vocal about it. I thought I was helping you, but my assessment of the situation was wrong. My intentions were noble; I wanted to protect you from an unequal marriage. I am sorry and only hope that after this meeting, we can still be friends."

"Darcy, I am speechless. All these months I have thought about her, about the decision I made. I know you and my sisters helped me make the decision, but if anybody is at fault; it is I. I should be my own man. I left the country without saying goodbye, and even before talking to her to see what her feelings were. I was also a coward, and maybe it is too late now. Besides, I am not sure if I should be seriously courting someone." Darcy remained quiet. He was convinced he had to confess and no more. After that, it was up to Bingley to act.

Chapter 6

At Longbourn, Elizabeth and Mrs Gardiner had already arrived and awaited news of the developments in London. The next day, an express from Mr Bennet arrived. As usual, he was very brief in his letter:

My dear wife and daughters,

Finally, we have found the fugitives.

I announce Lydia will be marrying Lieutenant WG on Friday.
I will be back to my family and books on Saturday.

Yours,
TB

Mrs Bennet was ecstatic about this news. "I knew it, she was getting married, and Mr Wickham would be a perfect son in law, so charming." Elizabeth felt sick; this was the end of all hope of a future with Fitzwilliam. Kitty pointed out that it was strange her father wrote WG and not GW. Jane mentioned that for sure, he was tired and just made a mistake while writing.

That evening Elizabeth asked her Aunt Gardiner to invite her again to travel with her to London. Her Aunt wanted to be as soon as possible back home, and they arranged their transportation for Friday. Elizabeth didn't want to arrive in time for the wedding. Mrs Gardiner knew the pain she was suffering and understood this but was sure that Mr Darcy and Elizabeth would find the way to be together. Madeleine knew how stubborn her niece was. It was better not to insist on this, at least not this time. She had also seen how determined Mr Darcy was as well. All would be well, she was convinced of it.

Before leaving, Elizabeth and Jane had one of their long conversations. Jane was convinced that Mr Darcy was doing all in his power to correct Lydia's wrong actions so he could soon marry her sister. She was impressed by Mr Darcy's steadfast love for her sister and had to compare it with Mr Bingley's actions. She didn't want in her life a fickle gentleman. She longed and needed a strong man beside her. She confessed to Elizabeth that now she was convinced Mr Bingley was not the right person for her. Jane wasn't sure to confess to her sister this thought. She knew how this matter had been an obstacle for Elizabeth to accept Mr Darcy.

Elizabeth was a very generous person and wise for her years. She accepted that at the time of the proposal, she acted based on the facts known at that moment, so she would not punish Jane for her change in heart. They embraced each other, and Jane insisted that Elizabeth might miss Mr Darcy if she went to London. Elizabeth didn't tell Jane nor her Aunt that she decided to leave England and Mr Darcy for good. She loved him so much that she could not bear to see him making the wrong decision. He would hate her for giving him hope and then disappearing from his life. It was cruel, but in the end, it would be best for him.

Friday morning was a fateful day for Lydia and Elizabeth. Lydia started her married life really happy, although she was disappointed about how quiet the ceremony and wedding breakfast were. Her husband was strict and had a way to control any outburst she might have by expressing that any pin money would be deserved. If not, he would retain it as long as her behaviour was childish. Until she proved otherwise, he would treat her like a child. It seems that what she needed was a determined guide, and she found him in Lieutenant Graham. Mr Bennet finished the wedding breakfast, very satisfied with the outcome for Lydia. He thought it would be a great joke when his family thought he miswrote the broom's initials in his short letter. They would be astonished when the young couple visited Longbourn on their way to Newcastle and meet WG, their new brother.

Upon arriving at the Gardiners, Elizabeth and her Aunt found that Mr Bennet had already left for Longbourn. He decided that it was still a good time in the afternoon to travel back home. The couple also departed for a short stay at Southampton, where his family lived. This was quite a relief for Elizabeth. She didn't want to face her father or her sister at the moment. She was disappointed with her father's lack of control over Lydia. She was still angry with Lydia for destroying her chance for happiness.

Elizabeth was unpacking, and in the other part of town, Mr Darcy was making all the arrangements for his departure. He planned to return to

Pemberley the following day, where he thought Elizabeth would be waiting for him. Darcy invited Richard, but the Colonel had to stay in London one week due to some duties at the War Office. He would reach them afterwards. Besides, Richard also wanted to go to Longbourn to assess the family. Darcy was his cousin and best friend, he was really like a brother, and he wanted to meet the Bennet household's other members. Richard promised to stand by him but to properly do so; it was needed to have a full understanding of all the family members. He quite liked Mr Bennet. His sarcastic sense of humour was much to his liking. Although he thought he lacked authority, at least in his youngest child's education, it was not right to judge him. He could imagine that having five daughters would be a daunting task, and it would be hard not to spoil them. He had a weak spot for Georgie, and she was just his cousin. He could imagine the kind of control a little girl of his own would have on him. Thank God he was still a bachelor. It was easier to command a regiment, he thought.

When the Colonel arrived at Longbourn, the house was in an uproar. They were all so satisfied with the fact that Lydia was found and safely married. The most astounding news was that their new brother was a real gentleman and not the rake they now knew Wickham to be. Mrs Bennet couldn't believe this news. When the Colonel entered the parlour, he was greeted with friendly smiles. Mr Bennet had already narrated the vital role he and Mr Darcy played in the scheme. He never mentioned to his wife and daughters anyhow, the amount of money Mr Darcy spent in it. That was Mr Darcy's only request to Mr Bennet, and after several hours of conversations, Mr Bennet relented.

Colonel Fitzwilliam immediately became a favourite of all with his charming and engaging conversation. He found the whole family very warm and friendly, but his eyes always seemed to seek Jane. *"Bingley is a fool, how could he have been persuaded to leave such a lady,"* he thought. The Colonel was a man of the world and had met many eligible women. Of course, he always had this theory that he needed a wealthy heiress. It was more a way to dissuade any interested ladies in him and to remain a bachelor longer. Until he saw Jane, this was the perfect argument. The serene and gentle spirit would soothe any pain he felt. During his military career, he experienced destruction, tragedy, and loss. He had a positive attitude in life. No one could suspect the deep pain he also carried, only Darcy knew about some of the nightmares he struggled with. The effect Jane had on him was something he never experienced before. Richard would have to tread carefully if she really had feelings for Bingley. He couldn't interfere with Darcy's friend, and he would not start a campaign knowing from the beginning that he would be the loser.

It was such a merry afternoon, and Mrs Bennet suggested a walk in the garden with the Colonel. He happily obliged and Jane and Mary went with him. Soon Mary was distracted with one of her favourite books. The Colonel had the chance to inquire after Mr Bingley discreetly. He was a strategist and knew several interrogation skills, which came in handy. He was able to discern that Jane didn't have a broken heart. It was the best news he could have received! He made up his mind to start his "campaign" to conquer the beautiful lady.

After returning from their walk, Mrs Bennet asked him about his travelling plans. He mentioned his plan to spend the night at the Meryton Inn, immediately Mr Bennet indicated that he should stay at Longbourn. After all the help of the Colonel with Lydia, Mr Bennet had a soft spot for this gentleman. Also, he would love to play chess with him; he was undoubtedly a challenging opponent. The Colonel was more than happy to oblige. He wanted to spend as much time as possible with the family. He had already confirmed that they would be a loving family for Darcy. Although Mrs Bennet was a little loud for his taste, he thought she was no different from many mothers of the ton. Most probably, she would be more tolerable after she saw her daughters well settled.

Dinner was delicious, and Mrs Bennet's table was exquisite. That was a pleasant surprise for the Colonel. He enjoyed good food and was impressed with the quality served at Longbourn. Mr Bennet's wit didn't disappoint either, and Jane's company made dinner more enjoyable. He would be happy to call Elizabeth "cousin", or even better, "sister". After dinner, the gentlemen retired to Mr Bennet's study to play chess. Before leaving the ladies, the Colonel mentioned to the room in general, always looking at Jane, he had to go the day after early in the morning. Jane immediately replied, not without blushing, that he should depart after having breakfast with the family. "Since you enjoyed Mamma's dinner so much, you just cannot miss her breakfast." He was glad to express his acceptance.

The next day after having breakfast, Jane mentioned that it was a pity he didn't have the chance to say hello to Elizabeth. He was confused now. Elizabeth was supposed to be in Pemberley with Georgiana since she was still recovering from the accident. Jane told him about her visit to Longbourn and her trip to London. The Colonel was preoccupied now since Darcy was probably reaching Pemberley quite soon. He was concerned about the reason for Elizabeth leaving Pemberley. And the consequences of this in the relationship with his cousin. Jane promised him she would try to help if necessary. With this promise and the invitation of Mrs Bennet to the Colonel, once he returned from his trip to Pemberley, he left Longbourn.

***

While Richard was meeting the love of his life, Darcy was arriving at Pemberley to find out that Elizabeth actually had left. "Brother, I am so happy you are back. I was waiting to receive a letter from you, and I actually wrote to you while you were in London, but you didn't reply. I think you were extremely busy." He was so shocked not to see his Elizabeth at home, he didn't respond to Georgiana's words for several minutes. She saw his disappointment and then remembered the letter she left for him. "Lizzy left this letter for you, I almost forgot." He was still confused and told Georgie he needed to take a bath, and they would meet afterwards.

He went to his room, but he wanted nothing more than to read what she wrote to him. After everything they had experienced, and what he had done for her family, he didn't expect her to leave. Something should be really wrong.

Dear Mr Darcy,

With a heavy heart, I write this letter to you.

You are so dear to me that I cannot bear to see you make a mistake. I have seen what you need in a wife and as the mistress of your estates. I could never be that person. You were right in April when you said to me that you were proposing to me "against your better judgment." I came to love you and will love you forever, but I cannot accept to destroy you, Georgie, and any children of yours. You deserve someone better. I am not enough. My family is a disgrace, and it is not fair for you to have such sisters and even worse, such a brother-in-law.

I hope someday you can forgive me.

You deserve to be happy. You are the best man I have ever known.

*Yours always,
Elizabeth*

"This is impossible. This could not be happening," Darcy thought. Elizabeth trusted him with Lydia's disgrace. Before he left Pemberley in search of her sister, she accepted to stay and wait for him. Something must have happened to make her change her mind so drastically. After taking a quick bath, he went to Georgie's music room. She was an exquisite interpreter, and it soothed his mind and soul to hear her. Georgiana sensed him and stopped playing. "Georgie, what happened? Why did she leave Pemberley?"

"I am not sure, Brother, but Lizzy was distraught after Lady Catherine's visit," Georgiana said.

"What? Lady Catherine was here? I don't understand what business would she have to come all the way from Kent?"

"She was very sly and stayed for only two days with us. She had a satisfied look when she left, that is why I wrote to you. I am sorry you didn't receive my letter."

He had to write to Richard, he couldn't reach Longbourn or London so soon. He had multiple affairs that needed immediate attention. Still, Richard could help him buy some time and at least find exactly where Elizabeth was. The soonest he could leave was eight days, and Richard was still in London since his duties at the War Office were taking longer than initially planned.

Of course, he would not allow Elizabeth to make such a terrible mistake. She was the only person right for him, as his wife and mistress of his estates. Even if Miss Lydia was still a disgraced lady, he would marry Elizabeth. Also, if Wickham would be his brother-in-law, he would marry Elizabeth. Darcy would not allow anyone to interpose between them. He had the support of his closest family members. Richard thought his parents would stand by him. The only person really against this marriage was his Aunt Catherine, but that was not an impediment at all. There would be some trials to adjust to the "ton", but that was nothing that someone as charming and intelligent as Elizabeth could not overcome. Besides, he now knew that he didn't care what the "ton" thought about his private life.

Dear Richard,

There is a matter of urgency in which you must help me.

I arrived earlier at Pemberley to find that Elizabeth was gone. I am sure our dear Aunt Catherine is behind all this. I don't know what lies she told her, and she left.

I cannot lose her again.

Unfortunately, the soonest I can leave is in eight days. In the meantime, could you please go check if Elizabeth is in London or Longbourn? Please tell her to give me a chance to talk to her.

Your brother,
FD

Once Richard received the express, he decided to visit the Gardiners. He knew the close relationship Elizabeth had with them. For sure, they would know about her whereabouts. "Colonel, how nice to see you again. Unfortunately, Mr Gardiner is not home," Mrs Gardiner said. She was such a fine lady, she reminded him of Jane.

"Mrs Gardiner, the pleasure is always mine. I hoped to see you today. You see, I think you are exactly the person who could help me." After having tea and some delicious scones, Richard had the information he needed. Although Elizabeth asked her Aunt not to tell her destination, Mrs Gardiner and Richard were allies in this endeavour.

"I have never seen Lizzy so helpless. There was nothing I could say to convince her to change her mind. Not even the fact that Mr Wickham would never be her brother-in-law. She was so adamant that she would not make Mr Darcy happy. You know how stubborn she can be. In the end, my husband had a business trip to his new Gardiner Emporium warehouse in Dublin. We both thought that a change of scenery would help her think things through. Lizzy is very good at organising the book collections, and this distraction will be positive, I am sure."

My favourite cousin,
I had a most enjoyable meeting with the gracious Mrs Gardiner.

Don't travel to London or Longbourn, and don't scowl when you read this sentence.

You should go to Dublin and search there for your ladylove.
She is helping her Uncle at Gardiner Emporium there.

You will succeed, as you always do when you put your mind to it.

Godspeed,
Richard

It was a balm to receive Richard's express so soon. It was also always gratifying to have his friendship and his sense of humour. It was unbelievable how Richard, after all the horror he had seen in war, still had such an attitude towards life. He also deserved happiness. He couldn't go back to the frontline; it would be insupportable for all the family. Richard had already sacrificed a lot and had been wounded several times. Maybe next time he wouldn't be so lucky. Darcy had already lost his parents, and now possibly Elizabeth, Darcy couldn't lose Richard. He would help him settle, one of the Darcy estates could suit him. Richard could learn to manage it, only if he could find the right woman to love. That would be a blessing. Little did Darcy know that the lady to help Richard resign to his military life was no other than Jane Bennet.

On his way to Pemberley, Richard decided to pay a visit to Longbourn. He couldn't stop thinking about the beautiful Jane Bennet. Once the Colonel arrived, he was greeted by the Bennet family and Bingley, who recently decided to return to Netherfield. He didn't expect a rival. He knew Mr Bingley was most likely to court Miss Bennet, but he would not be defeated without a fight. He knew from his previous conversation with Jane that she didn't love Bingley, and his hope increased when he saw the reaction she had when he greeted her. Jane blushed and swallowed hard while making a curtsey that didn't go unnoticed by the ever-observant Colonel. Mr Bingley was a little nervous after sensing the disapproval in the Colonel's eyes. The Colonel appreciated Bingley but always considered he still needed to mature. For him, Charles was still a boy. Jane needed a man, he was quite sure of it. After some awkward moments, Mr Bingley decided to leave. Jane eyed him with an assessing look. The Colonel didn't lose time and asked Mrs Bennet if someone would like to join him for a short walk. Kitty was in the middle of a drawing and didn't want to interrupt, but Jane and Mary were happy to walk again with the Colonel.

"It was quite a surprise to see Bingley back in Hertfordshire. I thought he would be releasing the lease." Jane replied that she didn't know about his plans, which always seemed to change without notice. This comment had an underlying message, the Colonel was sure. With this opening, he told her that he had thought about her. Jane blushed and bit her bottom lip. He could see he affected her but didn't know how she touched him. When she did that, he wanted to take her in his arms and kiss her. "Miss Bennet, I am an old man already, and since the first day I met you, I felt a connection with you. I will love to court you if you allow me. I want to get to know you better, so you can decide whether you could learn to love me. I know already what I feel for you, which only becomes stronger with time." Jane was speechless after these words. She saw both her suitors that day and could not avoid comparing them. She knew already that she was flattered by Bingley's attentions in autumn. Still, her heart was touched only by Richard Fitzwilliam. "I will love that, Richard." He couldn't stop from taking her in his arms and kiss her soundly.

Chapter 7

Ireland's beautiful landscapes were a blessing for Elizabeth. She had always dreamed about visiting the "Emerald Isle". She was an outdoor person, and green has always been her favourite colour. She also felt a special connection to the place. Her mother's family had relatives there. The country had a special magic, and she loved it at first sight. "Uncle, this is wonderful. I am so grateful that you invited me on this trip. I am sure I will love to live here."

"How could I deny you such an opportunity, you are special to us Lizzy, and we hate to see you so downcast. Besides, I think no one could help me arrange the book collection as well as you. We will enjoy our stay, I am sure."

Elizabeth was impressed with the location of the shop. 47 Lower Gardiner Street was the address, it couldn't be a coincidence. Actually, it wasn't. Luke Gardiner, 1st Viscount Mountjoy, who happened to be a cousin of Mr Gardiner, laid out in the 1709s this long Georgian street in Dublin. This street stretches from the River Liffey, and the Custom House terminates the vista at the southern end. It was fantastic, and

Elizabeth couldn't find a better place to start her new life. "Uncle, why didn't you tell me about the street name before, I am ecstatic! And my mother has never boasted about her noble relatives, how so?"

"Well, miracles happen! I wanted to see you smile, it has been a long time since you were looking so well, and I see I achieved it!"

They spent their days organising the book collection at the warehouse. Elizabeth also wanted to learn more about the business, and her Uncle was a great teacher. The shop he had there was adorable. He sold mainly books but also had an area where he sold tea, coffee, and fine chocolates. It wasn't too large, but it was welcoming. Elizabeth suggested they could make room to put four tables. The customers could also enjoy a cup of tea while looking at the books they were interested in purchasing. Her Uncle loved the idea! Elizabeth had decided she would never marry and wanted to be distracted and busy. She convinced his Uncle to let her manage the shop.

Although she was busy, she also dedicated some time to learn about the city. She loved to stroll through the streets, visit Dublin Castle, but her favourite was Phoenix Park. She was impressed with the Royal Canal construction, and some days she sat down to practise her drawing skills. It was a new activity for her but one that gave her peace. She would never forget her time at Pemberley. It was the happiest moment in her life, and she would treasure it always. She frequently thought about Georgiana, Mrs Reynolds, Dr Scott, and Paul. But mostly about the Master of Pemberley, who would remain in her mind and soul forever.

After ten hectic days, her Uncle had to return to England. She was sad to see him leave but was also thrilled with the new responsibility at the shop. She was starting a new chapter in life and felt she was up to the challenge. At the shop, she had a small but cosy office, where she could organise the book collections and review the accounts. The customers were served by Mr and Mrs O'Connell. They were a charming middle-aged couple with no children of their own. Mr O'Connell was very well-read, and she loved to hear his narrations about the history of the city and the country. She also liked to take a cup of tea at the end of the business day and read the letters from home.

Dear Lizzy,

You will not believe this news. I can hardly believe it myself.

You know the Colonel has been in Longbourn a couple of times. The last time he came, Mr Bingley was also here. I was so intimidated to have them both at the same time. You know Mr Bingley has been visiting already since last week. He is kind, but Lizzy, what I told you before is true. He didn't touch my heart. It was fantastic to receive his attentions. But I could not live with someone who was unable to say goodbye in person or didn't dare to ask me directly about my feelings. I was sad after last autumn but not because I was in love. I felt mistreated by the members of a family I thought were friends. Mr Bingley needs to mature and needs another kind of woman beside him. Lizzy, you will be happy to hear this. I cannot be Caroline's friend. She is not someone I would like to call "sister".

But coming back to the reason for this letter. I am being courted, Lizzy! Richard is the most wonderful gentleman of my acquaintance. I think I loved him since we first met. Isn't that strange? I know it sounds crazy, but it is true. Lizzy, I am travelling to London next week to meet his parents. He assures me, they will be thrilled. I hope it is so! I wish you were here with me to give me strength.

I will write soon,
Your loving sister,
Jane

Elizabeth was happy for her sister but couldn't avoid thinking she had made a big mistake. If her sister was enough to be the daughter in law of an earl, why couldn't she marry the love of her life? Elizabeth knew Lady Catherine's arguments were persuasive. Still, after reading this letter, she accepted that once again, she acted impulsively and made a rash decision.

She was anguished with the thought about all the mistreatment from her side. She refused Fitzwilliam once and fled when they reestablished their friendship and after everything he had done for her family. For sure, he would hate her ungratefulness. She acted harshly, and without giving the situation enough analysis, she lost her only chance for happiness.

She prayed he would forgive her in the future. Her most potent fear was losing his "good opinion". He told her his major fault was his "implacable resentment" and that once he lost his good opinion, there was no going back. She couldn't dare to meet him and see the disdain in his eyes. That would be unsupportable. *"Oh, but if Jane marries Richard, we will meet again. I cannot return to England. It is the only option,"* she thought.

***

Mr Darcy's departure to Ireland was delayed by an unexpected incident with one of Pemberley's neighbouring estates. It was already early September when his carriage arrived at Liverpool on a chilly but sunny day. He was never so nervous in his entire life. His fate would be sealed forever in this trip to Dublin.

He arrived at the Castle Hotel on Great Denmark Street, took a bath and decided that there was no other time like the present. They had already lost many months; he was determined to win her back as soon as possible. The weather was still lovely, and he opted to walk; it was only a ten-minute walk from his hotel to Lower Gardiner Street. There it was, GARDINER EMPORIUM BOOKS and MORE. He arrived at the shop and expected to see her immediately. He was disappointed to be received by an older gentleman. "I am looking for a unique jewel," said Mr Darcy.

"You might be in the wrong shop, Sir, we have books, some of them are quite the jewels of course, but besides books, we only sell coffee and tea, would you care to taste them? We have received excellent blends this week."

Mr Darcy was impatient, didn't want to waste time in small talk, but he also recognised a friendly face in Mr O'Connell. Besides, he couldn't risk his lack of cooperation; he needed all the allies he could get.

"Sir, I appreciate a good coffee, but I insist, you do have a jewel." Mr O'Connell was confused. After serving a very aromatic coffee cup to Mr Darcy, he decided to look for some help from Elizabeth to guide the noble-looking gentleman. He didn't want to insult such a potential customer.

Elizabeth was in her office at the back of the shop. "Miss Elizabeth, I would require your assistance, please. There is a gentleman who seems confused with what we have in the shop. I have mentioned to him that we don't have any jewels, but he insists. He looks imposing but also polite, and I would hate to lose such a special customer. Could you give me a hand? He is right now sampling our coffee."

Elizabeth was intrigued, that sounded strange. She went then to the shop counter to help Mr O'Connell. When she arrived, Mr Darcy sensed her, and they both stared at each other and remained speechless. After some minutes, Mr Darcy said, "Sir, as I mentioned to you, you do have a unique jewel in this shop."

Mr O'Connell felt Elizabeth's distress and was more concerned than anything. "Please, Sir, maybe it would be wise if you returned later?"

"I have waited for many weeks already, too many. Miss Elizabeth, could you spare me some time, we could talk over coffee?" Elizabeth reluctantly accepted.

"Sir, I am sorry you came all this way to talk about a future that cannot be. I hope you can forgive me someday." She had tears in her eyes but was able to maintain her composure.

"Elizabeth, I will not accept this answer and will always search for you. We belong together, and whatever my Aunt told you, it is nonsense."

"Your Aunt is right, I cannot bear to see you regret marrying me in some years, and that is what will happen." Mr Darcy was quick to deny that all these arguments were not real obstacles. He recognised that maybe some members of the ton would have issues accepting his choice, but didn't she know how steadfast his love was? Darcy had the support from the most important people in his life, Georgiana, Richard, Lord, and Lady Matlock. He didn't need anyone else's acceptance. Darcy was a respected gentleman in the ton and knew that Elizabeth would charm any deserving person. The rest, he didn't care about. And Richard was marrying Jane. His family already accepted her and were pleased to see the person Richard chose as his wife.

She was strong in her position until she saw him. Seeing him was something she could not resist. She started doubting her thoughts, and after he had come all this way just to see her and still didn't hate her for the suffering she had caused him. It was too much. She started crying, and he came to her and held her in his arms. They fit together perfectly; they were literally made for each other. Gently he touched her cheek and stopped some tears from falling. "My dearest Elizabeth, I love you, only you, now and forever." In her eyes, he found what he was looking for, a confirmation of her deep feelings for him. He was so overwhelmed by this meeting. Finally, seeing she was in front of him was too much to bear. He impulsively pulled her again into his arms, and in that embrace, he communicated all his love. She instinctively wrapped her arms around him and felt consumed by his dark eyes. He brushed his lips against hers, and when she slightly parted her lips, he couldn't resist and kissed her with a desperate need. "I have to tell you once again, how violently in love I am with you, would you do me the honour of being my wife? Accept my hand, since you already own my heart." That instant she recognised she couldn't deny him anything. With these thoughts, she barely noticed the velvet box Mr Darcy took from one of his pockets. "This belonged to my mother, she mentioned that I should give it to the woman I love."

"You were very sure of yourself, Mr Darcy."

"Elizabeth, we are past these formalities, please call me Fitzwilliam. And I wasn't sure of myself, I was never so nervous in my life, but I came prepared and was hopeful."

Elizabeth opened the black velvet box and saw an exquisite emerald ring surrounded by small diamonds. It delighted her heart!

"We have wasted too much time between my pride and your misconceptions. Let's marry here and soon, my love. I know you wish your family was here, but we can stay and explore this beautiful country. When we return to England, we can have a family celebration. Besides, Carton House is the estate *we* have in Maynooth, Kildare County and I haven't visited it in years. It is beautiful, you will love it."

"We?" she said.

"All I have is already yours. It will be an honour and a privilege to share everything with you, my loveliest Elizabeth."

"There is nothing in life I would like more. I thought you hated me, and I couldn't bear to see you looking at me differently. I don't deserve your love after the way I have treated you. I am so sorry. I would love to spend the rest of my life, showing you how much I love you. I hope someday I really deserve you, Fitzwilliam."

"Don't say that, my love. I can see how my words in Kent and what my Aunt told you have haunted you. You acted based on your tender feelings for Georgie and your love for me. It is because of the selflessness that you left us. Jane told Richard, and I could finally understand your decision to leave Pemberley. I had already decided I would do anything in my power to win your heart. I would never give up unless you told me you loved someone else."

They shared the happy news with the O'Connells. They toasted with a glass of excellent champagne. Mr Gardiner always kept some bottles at the shop for his most exclusive customers. Immediately, they started planning the coming days. Mr O'Connell knew the right clergyman for the ceremony. Elizabeth and Fitzwilliam wrote letters to their families to tell them the fantastic news.

Reverend Tackley could perform the ceremony in two days. Since Mr Darcy had a special licence, it was arranged without any problems. The most complicated thing was to have the wedding dress ready in such a short time. Mrs O'Connell knew the best modiste in town. Madame Lovett was happy to oblige. She usually acquired her fabrics from Mr Gardiner's business and could provide the dress in two days. Elizabeth was delighted to decide on her own what to wear for the occasion. Without her mother, she could choose a subtle style. Elizabeth actually loved the suggestion of not using a traditional bonnet. She would wear a delicate veil embroidered with small pearls.

In the meantime, Darcy was organising their wedding trip. They would spend the wedding night at the Castle Hotel. The next morning they would depart towards Carton House. On their way, they would stop at Lucan and stay there one night. He wrote to Lady Louisa Conolly, owner of Castletown and former friend of his mother, to see if they could stay there a couple of nights. He wasn't sure the family was in residence, but that could be a fantastic plan before continuing to Carton House. Lady Louisa was a forward-thinking woman. The initiatives and foundations to improve the lives of foundlings and vagabonds would be inspiring for Elizabeth.

September 12th, 1813, was the wedding day of Elizabeth and Fitzwilliam. It was a bright morning, and the ceremony started at eight o'clock in the morning. Mr Darcy had a reply to his express from Lady Conolly. Edward, the great-nephew of Lady Louise and friend of Darcy, was happy to assist as his best man. Elizabeth arrived on time with the O'Connells. Mr O'Connell was proud to walk with Elizabeth. Once Darcy saw her at the church's door, he was stunned. His eyes were for her only. She was absolutely beautiful in her refined ivory dress. He loved the fact she didn't wear a bonnet. He loved to see her face and hair, and the veil was very delicate and almost transparent. He hardly paid attention to the Reverend. He came from his stupor when they were pronounced husband and wife. Finally, Elizabeth was "his wife".

The End

Acknowledgements

I want to thank Federico Tamayo for his excellent help with the design of the book cover and to the editing team at Self-Publishing Services and last but not least, thanks to Jane Austen for still being a source of inspiration.

Made in the USA
Columbia, SC
07 October 2020